Forward*

The inspiration for this story came from my friend Ruth Philips, when a stray chicken came to her house. Most of the story here is true. The chicken is now a pet, with very good care.

Illustrations by the author.

*Find the 20 crosses (+) throughout the story.

The Brave Little
Red Chicken

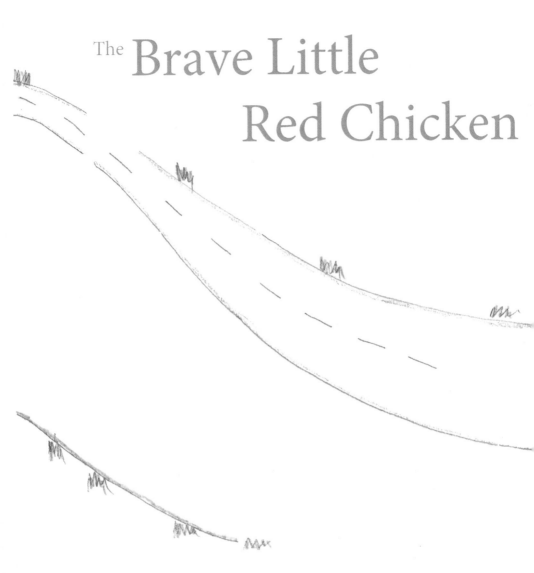

Once upon a time, a chicken family
decided to go to town.

While going down the highway, the little red chicken (that's me) slipped through the cracks and fell to the ground along the side of the road.

Oh my! What will I do? I thought to myself.

My family is gone! Maybe they will find me on their way back home. But I never saw them again.

There was a nice looking house along the road. So I decided to stay around, and hoped I could find something good to eat.

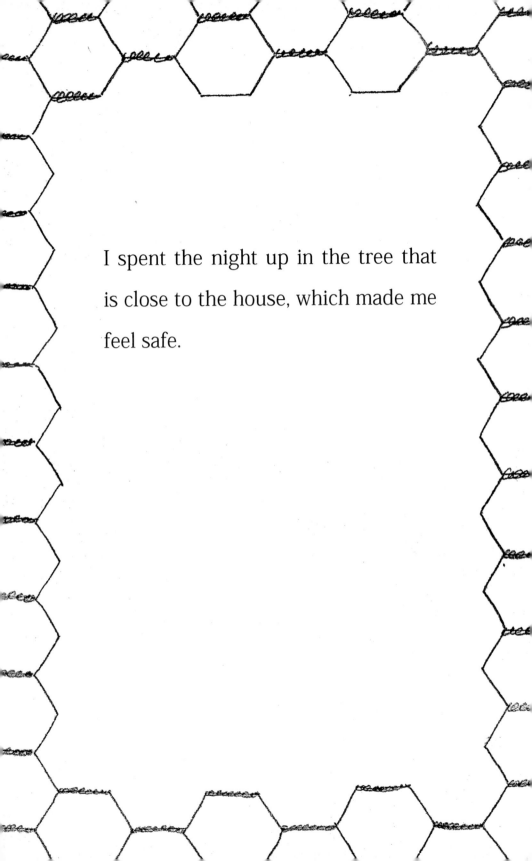

I spent the night up in the tree that is close to the house, which made me feel safe.

Up in my tree house, I could look into the big picture window. I saw a little old lady inside, busying herself doing all kinds of things. This was very entertaining to me.

Sometimes there were many little old ladies in the house. All of a sudden, these people would all get up and look out the window at me. That made me feel very important.

I learned this little old lady's name was Ruthie. Ruthie named me Henny-Penny. That is such a pretty name for me. She gives me food and water, which makes me think she loves me.

I heard Ruthie talking on the phone "Yak-yak-yackety-yak!" to see if anyone had lost a chicken. I kinda like my home, and hoped Ruthie would not find another place for me.

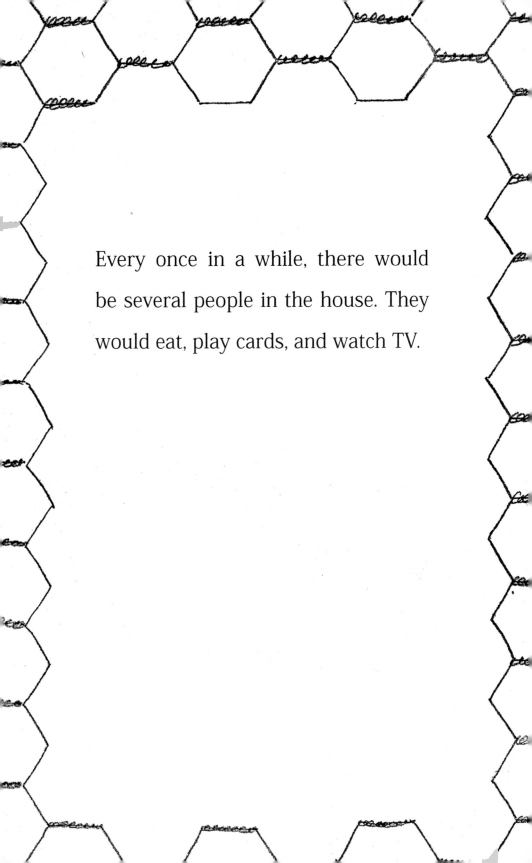

Every once in a while, there would be several people in the house. They would eat, play cards, and watch TV.

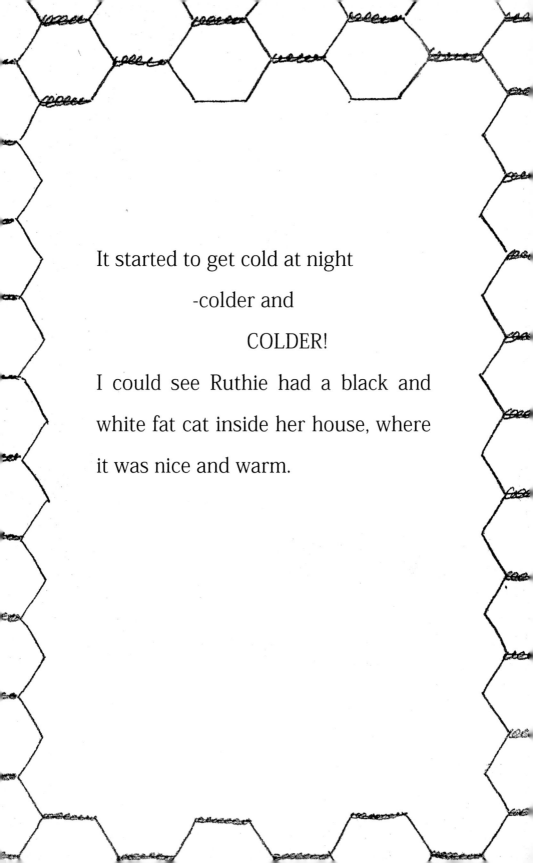

It started to get cold at night

-colder and

COLDER!

I could see Ruthie had a black and white fat cat inside her house, where it was nice and warm.

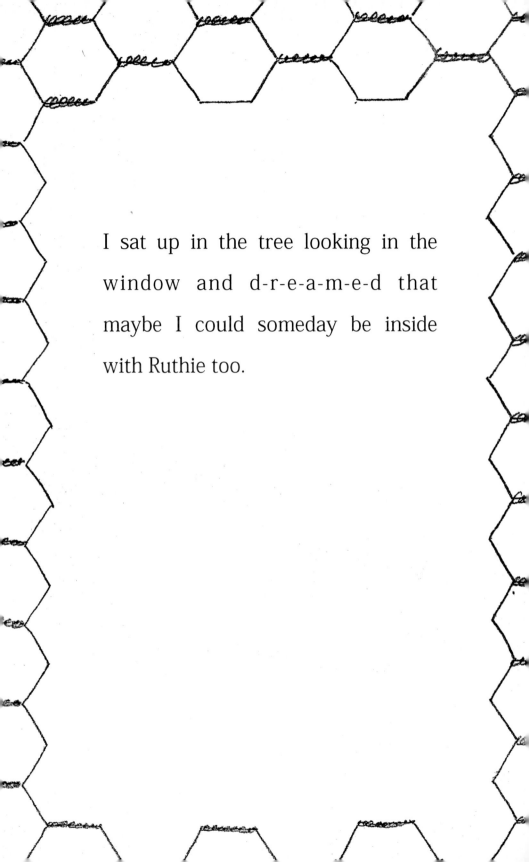

I sat up in the tree looking in the window and d-r-e-a-m-e-d that maybe I could someday be inside with Ruthie too.

When it started to get <u>really</u>-<u>really</u>-**<u>really</u>** cold, it started to snow. Ruthie is thinking how cold I'm getting outside. One evening, when it was nasty and bitter cold, I thought it would be warmer if I spent the night on the window sill.

Ruthie had a man named Larry come and put me in an outbuilding. It wasn't in Ruthie's house, but it sure was a lot better than staying outside in the cold weather. Ruthie buys me the best food and mealy worms to eat, and plenty of water everyday in my house. She makes me feel warm and loved.

Ruthie loves me so much, she kept me in the building all winter because she didn't want anything to happen to me. Spring came; and one day I promised little old Ruthie that I wouldn't run away. I would stay close to the house. Now Ruthie lets me out in the yard in the afternoon. I get to run around in the yard, play, eat bugs and grass. When it starts to get dark, I go back in my house and settle down for the night, just as I promised Ruthie I would do. Ruthie comes and closes the door so I will be safe.

I'm so glad I found such a wonderful home!

Ruthie would come and feed me everyday. I would sing her the best song I know how to sing. "Cluck-a-dee-dee-a-dee-dee! Cluck-a-dee-dee-a-dee-dee! I love little ole' Ruthie for taking good care of me!" I would even let Ruthie pet me.

Since Ruthie takes such good care of me, and we get along so well, I wanted to do something very special for her. I thought, and thought, and thought. What can I do for her? She has everything in the house. After a long-long-long time, I finally decided what I would do. Yes, I laid her an egg!

When Ruthie came to feed me the next morning, little old Ruthie was sooooo surprised! She clapped, clapped, clapped her little old hands, and told me how happy I made her. Now I've decided to give her an egg every day. She tells me how good they are to eat. She even shares them with her friends. That just makes my little chicken heart feel so happy!

The End!

81662006R00022

Made in the USA
Lexington, KY
19 February 2018